For Pat, patron saint of illustrators—
maker of careers, banisher of doubts, and provisioner of brownies.

With gratitude to the Smithie Parents for sharing their
children's beautiful and inspiring artwork, and special thanks to
Adelaide A., Adelaide R., August, Mary, Noah, and Willow.

Dial Books for Young Readers
An imprint of Penguin Random House LLC, New York

First published in the United States of America by Dial Books for Young Readers,
an imprint of Penguin Random House LLC, 2021

Copyright © 2021 by Lisa Anchin

Dial & colophon are registered trademarks of Penguin Random House LLC.

Visit us online at penguinrandomhouse.com.

Library of Congress Cataloging-in-Publication Data is available.

Manufactured in China • ISBN 9780593110225 • 10 9 8 7 6 5 4 3 2 1

Design by Mina Chung • Text set in Monticello LT Pro

The publisher does not have any control over and does not assume any
responsibility for author or third-party websites or their content.

The art for this book was created with acryla gouache, colored pencil,
pencil, and collage.

The Paper Bird

Lisa Anchin

Dial Books for Young Readers

There once was a time when all of the colors, from midsummer blue to sunrise orange, lived at the tips of Annie's fingers.

They came whenever she called, and arrived in brilliant flashes of joy, singing and dancing across the page.

Then, on a Wednesday like any other, something changed.

For the first time, Annie heard the low giggles
and saw the sneaky looks.

The colors seemed to sing more quietly,
and without their bright voices,

gray doubt slowly crept in.

As the gray clouded in overhead, Annie noticed that the bird she was drawing looked more like a flying hippopotamus. She tried to banish it with her eraser, but it only made things worse.

Annie pulled out a new sheet of paper,
but the white page seemed impossible.

The more Annie tried to draw,
the grayer she felt.

The gray feeling lingered longer and longer,
and soon it spilled out everywhere.

By the end of the day,
Annie felt gray all over.

Instead of heading home with her classmates,
Annie snuck outside to the schoolyard and let the
quiet of the empty playground settle around her.

The quiet made Annie feel a little less gray, so she pulled a blank page from her backpack. She tried to draw the bird once more, but even here, the lines still wouldn't come out right.

Annie tried again and again and again,
but it seemed the gray had followed her.

Suddenly with a crinkle and a
whistle, her turquoise bird peeled
itself from the paper.

Annie looked at it in dismay; the bird was lopsided
with one wing longer than the other. She leaped up
to catch it before anyone caught sight of her mistakes.

Annie jumped and grabbed for the paper bird, but as it flew upward,
she paused. All she could see from her place on the ground was a
glorious trail of turquoise swooping and loop-de-looping above her.

The bird opened its beak and chirped a merry tune. The bright, cheery notes filled her with hope. Annie couldn't help herself. She decided to try a little yellow.

And red. And violet. And orange.

Every so often, Annie looked around, and when she was certain no one was watching, she painted more birds. Slowly the sky filled with birdsong and the rustle of painted wings.

Annie was so entranced by the sunny voices and swooping colors, she didn't notice what was happening to her discarded pages.

She looked up to find that the schoolyard
had disappeared in a forest of white. The trees
shushed and rustled. They crackled and snapped.
They were all made of paper!

The bright, bare paper trees called to Annie. She had never seen anything as beautiful and filled with possibility. Annie's eyes sparkled. The woods were hers and only hers. She reached again toward the bright paper trunks, the colors crackling at her fingers.

Annie whooped and hollered, and she painted the paper woods. There was no one watching, and it wouldn't have mattered if there were. Annie had found her colors.

At last she felt
like herself again.

The next day, when Annie stepped through the school gate, the paper woods were already gone.

But Annie had brought her colors with her, and back at school, they slowly began to spread.

There once was a time
when Annie knew only gray.

Lately, though, she strode with purple confidence,
sang with orange glee, and danced a golden streak of joy,

and she lived all the colors in between.